Dear Reader,

This book was made completely by me, Jake Cake. I did all the words and all the pictures and it took me ages. It's about all the strange things that get me into trouble. Strange things that are SO STRANGE no one EVER believes me.

When I try telling grown-ups what REALLY happened they shake their heads and say: 'DON'T MAKE UP STORIES OR YOUR NOSE WILL GROW LONG!' But I'm not making up stories. Everything I'm about to tell you is true. It all REALLY HAPPENED!

signed Jake Cake

Michael Broad spent much of his childhood gazing out of the window imagining he was somewhere more interesting.

Now he's a grown-up Michael still spends a lot of time gazing out of the window imagining he's somewhere more interesting – but now he writes and illustrates books as well.

Some of them are picture books, like *Broken Bird* and *The Little Star Who Wished*.

Books by Michael Broad

JAKE CAKE

THE PIRATE CURSE

Michael Broad

PUFFIN

This book is dedicated to my friend Michael.M

PUFFIN BOOKS

Published by the Penguin Group
Penguin Books Ltd, 80 Strand, London WC2R 0RL, England
Penguin Group (USA) Inc., 375 Hudson Street, New York, New York 10014, USA
Penguin Group (Canada), 90 Eglinton Avenue East, Suite 700, Toronto, Ontario, Canada M4P 2Y3
(a division of Pearson Penguin Canada Inc.)
Penguin Ireland, 25 St Stephen's Green, Dublin 2, Ireland (a division of Penguin Books Ltd)
Penguin Group (Australia), 250 Camberwell Road, Camberwell, Victoria 3124, Australia
(a division of Pearson Australia Group Pty Ltd)
Penguin Books India Pvt Ltd, 11 Community Centre, Panchsheel Park, New Delhi – 110 017, India
Penguin Group (NZ), 67 Apollo Drive, Rosedale, North Shore 0632, New Zealand
(a division of Pearson New Zealand Ltd)
Penguin Books (South Africa) (Pty) Ltd, 24 Sturdee Avenue, Rosebank, Johannesburg 2196, South Africa

Penguin Books Ltd, Registered Offices: 80 Strand, London WC2R 0RL, England

puffinbooks.com

First published 2008
3

Copyright © Michael Broad, 2008
All rights reserved

The moral right of the author/illustrator has been asserted

Set in Perpetua
Made and printed in England by Clays Ltd, St Ives plc

British Library Cataloguing in Publication Data
A CIP catalogue record for this book is available from the British Library

ISBN: 978-0-141-32369-5

www.greenpenguin.co.uk

Penguin Books is committed to a sustainable future
for our business, our readers and our planet.
The book in your hands is made from paper
certified by the Forest Stewardship Council.

Here are three UNBELIEVABLE stories about the times I met:

I was leaving school on Friday
afternoon, minding my own
business, when suddenly I got ambushed
at the gates!

'COOEEE! ANGEL CAKE!' Mum
shrieked, planting a big kiss on my

cheek in front of all my classmates. If that wasn't bad enough, she then dragged me off to go shopping!

A surprise school-gate ambush usually means shopping for clothes, shopping for shoes, or even worse – shopping for UNDERWEAR!

Underwear Shopping

ARRRGGH!

But luckily, this shopping trip had nothing to do with me. Mum had just picked me up from school because she was running late.

'We're going to the antique shop to look at a rather nice vase I've had my eye on,' Mum explained. 'So I don't want any trouble or made-up stories about haunted rocking horses or any other nonsense.'

'Yes, Mum,' I sighed, even though the haunted rocking horse wasn't made up. It went on the rampage last time Mum dragged me around an antique shop, but I'll tell you about that another time.

Mum likes collecting antiques, even though Dad calls them 'overpriced junk', and as we stepped inside the rickety old shop I had to agree with Dad. The shop was crammed full of dusty wooden furniture piled up with old clocks and lamps and ugly china ornaments.

'There it is!' Mum gasped. 'Isn't it *beautiful*?' I frowned at the lumpy green vase and was wondering whether or not to tell Mum it looked like a big bogey when a scruffy-looking man leapt out of nowhere and grabbed my wrists!

'Sticky fingers?'
he hissed, turning
my hands over to
inspect them. 'Are
you planning to plant
mucky fingerprints
all over my precious
antiques?'

'It's OK, Mr
Crooke,' Mum chuckled. 'This is my
son, Jake.'

'Ah, Mrs Cake!' said the man, as I
snatched my hands back and shoved
them in my pockets. 'You can never be
too careful with children's mucky paws.
They touch everything!'

'You're quite right, Mr Crooke!' said
Mum, and then went on to reassure the

scruffy old
man that I
would behave
myself in his
scruffy old
shop. I was
getting bored
with the
conversation

going on over my head when I noticed
a sign at the back of the shop that said
Treasure Chests.

Hmmm, I thought.

Mum and Mr Crooke moved over to
the bogey-vase so I grabbed my chance
and snuck away through the maze of
furniture and into the treasure-chest
section. But what Mr Crooke called

treasure chests was *actually* just a hoard of tatty wooden boxes.

'Overpriced junk,' I mumbled.

I was about to leave when I glimpsed something dull and brassy at the back of the room and stepped through the stacks of boxes to investigate. There I found a *proper* treasure chest with a curved top, brass edges and barnacles stuck all over it!

'Now *that's* more like it!' I gasped. Because barnacles mean ships, and ships mean pirates, and pirates mean treasure!

I kneeled down and brushed the dust and cobwebs from the front to reveal the words 'Old Crusty' carved into the wood in old-fashioned lettering. There was no lock on the chest, but when I tried to lift the lid it was stuck fast and didn't budge a millimetre.

I tapped the back, nudged the edges and heaved the lid again, but it was as if the whole thing had been welded shut.

KICK

OLD
CR

KICK!

I stood up and looked around, just to make sure creepy Mr Crooke hadn't crept up behind me, then I swung my right leg and gave the chest an almighty kick.

The lid immediately flew open with a massive windy WHOOOOOSH!

The wind knocked me off my feet and on to the dusty floor, and when I looked up I saw a huge pirate towering above me! He was a little bit see-through, which meant he was probably a ghost, but that didn't make him any less fierce and scary.

'WHO DARES TO STEAL ME TREASURE?'  he boomed, waving a sword in one hand and a hook in the other – actually the hook *was* his other hand.

'WHOEVER YE BE – YE HAVE AWAKENED THE CURSE OF OLD CRUSTY! OO-ARRH!'

The pirate wore an eye patch and was peering around the stacked boxes with his good eye, which couldn't have been *that* good because he still hadn't seen

me. In the chest below him I could see a
huge pile of gold coins.

'Where be ye hiding, coward?' he
snarled, baring his blackened teeth.

The pirate's weary-looking
parrot shuffled along his
shoulder, whispered
in his ear and jabbed
his beak in my
direction. Then
Old Crusty looked
down and saw
me sprawled
on the floor.

'Why, it be nought but a shrimpy
tadpole!' said the pirate, with a
disappointed frown. 'What say ye,
Shrimpy Tadpole?'

'Hello?' I said, because I didn't know
what else to say.

'Be ye after Old Crusty's treasure?'
he demanded, jabbing his sword at the
coins in the chest.

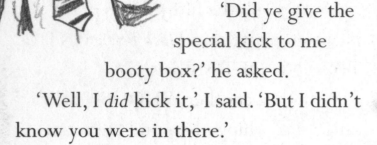

'Er, no,' I lied.
'Not really . . .'
'Did ye give the
special kick to me
booty box?' he asked.

'Well, I *did* kick it,' I said. 'But I didn't
know you were in there.'

'It matters not what ye know,
Shrimpy Tadpole!' said the
pirate. 'Ye have awakened
the curse of Old Crusty.
Scourge of the six seas –'

The parrot
rolled its eyes and
whispered in the
pirate's ear again.

– 'scourge of
the *seven* seas!'

Crusty corrected. 'Ye will be visited tonight and every night thereafter, and made to scrub the filthy decks of the phantom pirate ship *Black Bessie* UNTIL THE END OF TIME!'

With this, another WHOOSH of salty wind whipped around the room, Old Crusty was sucked back into the treasure chest and the lid slammed shut behind him. I was about to heave a sigh of relief when I noticed the WHOOSH

of salty wind had unsettled the stacks of boxes, which were now swaying back and forth above me, until . . .

CRASH!

They all came tumbling down around me, and the racket of falling boxes was followed by the sound of two sets of angry footsteps charging through the shop. Then I heard two outraged voices. One was yelling 'WHAT ON EARTH!' and the other was yelling 'STICKY FINGERS!'

Mum sent me to bed early that
night, but not before giving me a long
lecture about making up pirate stories.
She also told Dad that it was my fault
we didn't have a beautiful new vase
for the mantelpiece. Dad nodded
sympathetically, but I could tell he was
secretly pleased.

I was lying in bed and worrying
about the curse of Old Crusty when it
occurred to me that if the pirate couldn't

find me in the shop without help from the parrot, he probably wouldn't be able to find my house either.

Our cat Fatty waddled into my room and hissed at me. Fatty doesn't like me and usually likes to gloat when I'm in trouble, but then I noticed he wasn't hissing at *me* – he was hissing at the empty space at the end of my bed.

Fatty Hissing ←

A familiar salty wind whipped around the room as Old Crusty rose up at the base of my bed, waving his sword and hook. 'YE HAVE AWAKENED THE CURSE OF OLD

CRUSTY, SCOURGE OF THE EIGHT SEAS –'

The parrot made a movement towards the pirate's ear and then froze when he saw Fatty behind him, licking his lips and getting ready to pounce.

Fatty never does anything energetic,
unless there's food involved, so he must
have shot through the air
thinking his efforts would be
rewarded with a nice
colourful bird
to eat.

The parrot
didn't move as
the hissing ball of fur
sailed towards him and
continued not to
move as Fatty passed
right through his
feathered
body,

landing in a fat heap on my bed.

The parrot and the pirate looked quite amused when Fatty bounced off the bed with a thud and stomped out of the room. I chuckled too, until I remembered I had a pirate curse to deal with.

Old Crusty scratched his head with the hook. OUCH! And then picked up where he'd  left off. 'YE HAVE AWAKENED THE CURSE OF OLD CRUSTY, SCOURGE OF THE NINE SEAS –' at which point the parrot sighed heavily.

'Um, Mr Crusty?' I said, keen to skip another reading of the curse.

'*Captain* Crusty!' corrected the pirate. 'Old Crusty to me mateys.'

'Sorry. Captain Crusty?' I said.

'Yes, young Shrimpy Tadpole?'

'Um, I was just wondering about the curse,' I said. 'It's just that I haven't *technically* stolen your treasure because it's still in your chest. And I'm sorry I woke you up, but I was bored because my mum took me to the antique shop.'

'Arr, I knows about boredom, young Shrimpy Tadpole,' said the pirate, scratching his beard with the hook. OUCH! Again. 'I've been waiting in that trunk for over three hundred years, and most of that time was under water!'

The parrot nodded slowly to indicate that he found it boring too.

'Er, why?' I asked. 'Couldn't you just do something else?'

'But who would guard me treasure?' Old Crusty gasped.

'Well,' I said, and I tried to say what

I was going to say carefully. 'You don't actually *need* the treasure any more, do you? Being dead and all. It's not as though you could do anything with it.'

'But what would I do instead?' he said. 'I'm a pirate! All I knows is the sea.'

I thought about it for a minute, wondering what I'd do if I was a ghostly pirate with nothing to do. And then I had an idea.

'You could haunt a speedboat!' I said excitedly. 'Or a really fast yacht!'

Old Crusty put his sword away and sat on the end of the bed. 'Tell me about speedboats and yachts, young Shrimpy Tadpole,' he said, with a mischievous black-toothed grin.

I was up half the night chatting with
Old Crusty, explaining about speedboats
and yacht races, and everything else
I thought a three-hundred-year-old
pirate might need to know. He
was amazed at how fast boats
can go these days, and
the parrot flapped his
wings excitedly.

Then Old Crusty told
me what it was *really* like
to be a pirate.

As well as sailing
the *seven* seas, stealing
jewels and gold coins, they
also looted ships transporting
chocolate from the
Americas – which
definitely explained the
blackened teeth!

Old Crusty obviously missed being a pirate, but he was also very keen to give speedboats and yachts a go! Then he told me all about the treasure in his chest and how the curse could only be broken if someone claimed the booty.

'So ye must open the chest one more time, young Shrimpy,' he said.

'That might be a bit tricky,' I replied.

'. . . and I'm just too embarrassed to show my face there again,' Mum said firmly the next day.

'But what about the bogey – I mean, beautiful green vase?' I said.

Mum paused for a moment and looked at the empty space on the mantelpiece. It was the first time she'd wavered all morning and I knew it was time to play my ace card.

'And while we're there I can apologize properly and tidy up the mess I caused,' I said, and to seal the deal I smiled innocently and imagined a halo glowing over my head.

There was no sign of Mr Crooke when we entered the antique shop, so I quickly weaved through the maze of furniture. I was heading straight for the treasure chests when the shopkeeper leapt out of nowhere again, but this time he was waving a crowbar in the air!

'ARRRGH!' I screamed and froze to the spot.

'There you are, Mr Crooke!' Mum said, weaving through the furniture behind me. 'Jake has come to apologize for the incident yesterday and to tidy up any mess he caused.'

'That won't be necessary,' snapped Mr Crooke, folding his arms to block my way. 'Good day, Mrs Cake.'

'Oh.' Mum frowned. 'But I would still like to buy that beautiful vase –'

'It's not for sale any more!' Crooke interrupted rudely. 'Good *day*!'

'Well, really!' Mum gasped, and
stormed off towards the door. 'Come
on, Jake, we're leaving!'

I was still eyeing up the dodgy
shopkeeper and trying to work out what
he was up to, because I was pretty sure
he was up to *something*. Then my eyes
fell on the crowbar and I noticed there

was a bit of barnacle stuck
on the end.

BIT
OF
BARNACLE

'You're trying to open
Old Crusty's treasure chest!' I gasped,
as Mr Crooke quickly tucked the
crowbar behind his back. 'Well, *I*
already opened it yesterday by accident
and a crowbar won't do it.'

'That's impossible!' hissed Mr
Crooke. 'I've been working
on it for years!'

'It's stuffed full of gold
coins,' I added.

'Those coins
are mine!' Mr
Crooke growled.
'How did you open
it?'

'I'm not sure I *should* tell you after you were so rude to my mum,' I said, folding my arms. 'Which is a shame, because she really does like that horrible bogey-vase —'

'MRS CAKE!' squealed Mr Crooke, hurrying over to the counter. He grabbed the bogey-vase, wrapped it in newspaper and handed it to Mum with a cheesy grin. 'To apologize for my *appalling* manners.'

'Oh, I couldn't possibly,' Mum said, while still reaching for the parcel.

'I insist!' he blurted. 'Your son apologized *so* convincingly for the trouble yesterday, he quite won me over! So let's put it all behind us and say no more about it.'

'Really?' Mum said, smiling at me. 'And you don't need help cleaning up the mess he made?'

'Now that you mention it,' said Mr Crooke,

pretending to remember something. 'I could use a hand for a moment with *one* of

the boxes, if that's all right with you, of course?'

Mum nodded eagerly and began pulling at the paper parcel to peer at the bogey-vase.

Old Crusty's treasure chest was exactly where I'd left it, so I strolled over and gave it a swift kick. The  lid immediately flew open with a massive WHOOOOOSH! Then the salty whirlwind whipped around the room again and Old Crusty rose up from the gold coins.

39

'WHO DARES TO STEAL ME TREASURE?' he boomed, waving his sword through the air. 'WHOEVER YE BE . . .' The pirate paused as the parrot whispered in his ear again. 'Well, shiver me timbers! It be young Shrimpy Tadpole!'

'Hello, Captain Crusty,' I said.

'*Old* Crusty!' he corrected, with a black, toothy smile. 'Ye be a true matey for coming back to help this salty old sea dog!'

I nodded proudly, thinking how cool it was to be a real pirate matey.

'And who be this gawping barnacle-brain?' asked the pirate, pointing the sword at the startled shopkeeper. In all the excitement I'd forgotten about Mr

Crooke, who was staring at Old Crusty
with wide eyes and an even wider
mouth.

'P-p-pirate!' he burbled, and then
dribbled down his chin.

'He's here to claim your booty,' I said.
'If you don't mind?'

'It be no good to me now,' laughed
the pirate. 'And as ye told me last night

that ye have no use for it, then it may as
well go to this big dribbling jellyfish.'

I tried not to laugh at the names
he was calling Mr Crooke and waved
goodbye as the whirlwind whipped
up again and took Old Crusty and his
faithful parrot out through the ceiling.
I was sad to see them go, but
glad they weren't stuck inside
the chest any more.

With the pirate gone, Mr
Crooke quickly gathered
himself together and
barged past
me to get to
the treasure.
He sank to his
knees and

stared greedily at the glistening gold.

'Are you ready, Jake?' Mum called from the shop.

'Coming,' I said, and waited a moment longer to watch Mr Crooke plunge his hands into the chest of coins – because that's what people *always* do with a chest full of treasure.

SQUELCH!

Mr Crooke's greedy grin quickly became a grim grimace as the gold foil flaked away between his fingers and his hands came out covered in chocolate! Three-hundred-year-old chocolate that had come all the way from the Americas!

'*Chocolate* coins!' growled the greedy shopkeeper.

'Sticky fingers?' I chuckled, and then legged it.

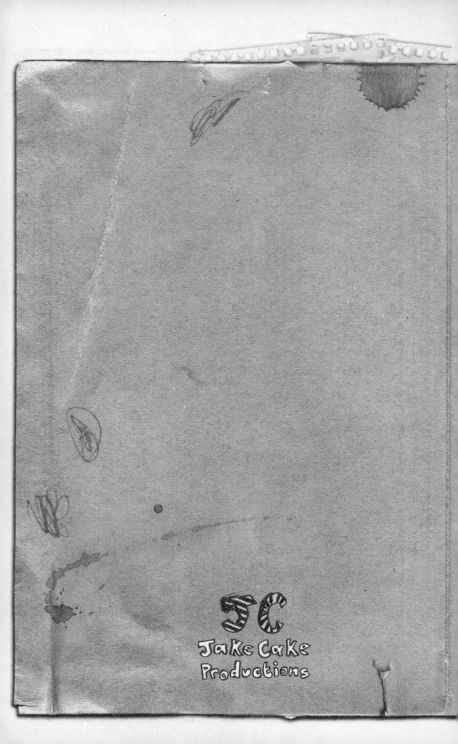

JC
Jake Cake
Productions

My granny is pretty cool – for a grown-up. She's my mum's mum, but unlike Mum she loves hearing all about my unbelievable adventures and *never* says my nose will grow long. Granny also makes a huge fuss of me,

GRANNY'S HERE!

so when I heard she was
coming to visit I was really
looking forward to it.

'Granny's here!' Mum
yelled, as the doorbell
rang.

I bolted downstairs
and ran to the front door
just as Mum opened it.

Usually it takes Granny a while to
get through the front door
because she starts making
a fuss of me straight away,
ruffling my hair
and saying
how tall I've
grown. But
this time she

burst through the door,
barged past me and
plonked herself firmly
in the armchair.

'Hello, Granny!' I
said, bracing myself to
be praised and ruffled.

'Hello . . .' Granny paused,
eyed me up and down
and added,
'little boy.'
It was
then that
I knew
something
strange was
going on

because Granny always calls me Jakey.

Even when I complain
and say I'm too grown
up to be called
Jakey, she still
calls me Jakey.
Mum and
Dad didn't
notice. Actually Dad
had made himself scarce as he always
does when Granny comes to visit, and
Mum was too busy talking at a hundred
miles an hour.

I sat on my beanbag
and stared
at the old
woman,
searching
for clues.

Was she really my granny, or someone pretending to be her?

She did look and sound like Granny, so she could just have been tired from the journey or having an off day. But I was so sure that Granny wasn't Granny I decided to test her.

'Granny,' I said, when Mum left the room to make a pot of tea, 'do you remember the time I met a zombie at the zoo and he was stealing the meat from the lion enclosure?'

HO! HO! HO!

'Yes, very amusing,' said Granny. 'Ho! Ho! Ho!'

The laugh was definitely suspicious;

it sounded like a robot Santa Claus!

'And the lions chased after him and ate him,' I added, narrowing my eyes.

'Of course,' said Granny. 'Naughty lions!'

Aha! I thought. Because it wasn't a zombie at all, it was a Viking, and the lions did chase him but he got away. We ended up having a barbecue behind the gorilla cage – but I'll tell you about that another time. Anyway, Granny would have remembered because, of all my adventures, the Viking at the zoo was her favourite.

'You're NOT my granny!' I said firmly.

'Uh?' said the granny impostor.

'It was a Viking!' I said. 'And *my* granny would have known that!'

'Oh yes! I remember now,' said the old woman. 'A Viking ate the zombie!'

'No!' I said, getting annoyed. 'A

Viking stole the meat and *no one* got eaten!'

'Yes, of course,' she said, looking a bit worried.

Mum entered the room with Granny's tea and I leapt up from my beanbag.

'THIS WOMAN IS AN *IMPOSTOR*!' I yelled, jabbing a finger at the floral-clad fake.

Mum calmly passed the old woman her tea and rolled her eyes dramatically. 'See what happens when you encourage him, Mum?' she said, shaking her head sadly. 'It's one silly story after another. Only last night he said a *flying saucer* landed in the back garden!'

'But there *was* a flying saucer!' I pleaded. 'It landed on the lawn and scuttled into the woods on three metal legs . . .'

The old woman's teacup rattled

nervously
in her
non-
flying
saucer and

I realized the two things
had to be connected.
Aliens dress up as humans
all the time in movies
— which completely makes

NON-FLYING
SAUCER

sense because they wouldn't get very far
looking all thin and green with big black
eyes.

'It was *her* flying saucer!' I gasped.
'She's an ALIEN GRANNY!'

The alien granny sipped from her
teacup and peered innocently up at

Mum. But Mum was too busy glaring at me, red-faced and snorting through her nostrils – and looking more like an alien than the alien.

'GO TO YOUR ROOM IMMEDIATELY!' she yelled.

In my room I searched the web for information on aliens. There was lots of stuff about UFO sightings and then I found a site that said aliens like to pluck cows out of fields, study them and then plonk them back again.

I can't imagine why an alien would want to study a cow because cows are really boring, but it gave me an idea. If I could get the bogus granny to do something alien, like studying cattle, she'd be completely busted.

The nearest thing to a cow I had was my cat, Fatty. He's very lazy, but he's still probably more interesting than a cow, so I knew the alien wouldn't be able to resist studying him.

FATTY GLARING

Fatty was glaring at me from the laundry bin in the corner of my room,

but not because he knew I planned
to use him as bait. Fatty *always* glares
because he's a grumpy old
cat who hates everyone.

I struggled downstairs,
holding Fatty at arm's

length as
he hissed
and spat
and swiped
wildly with
his claws.

But when
we reached the living room he stopped
struggling and frowned at the old
woman.

'I thought I told you to go to your
room!' Mum said crossly.

'Er, I've thought about what I said and have come to apologize to Granny,' I explained, and quickly shifted my face into an expression that I hoped looked sorry. 'And I've brought Fatty down because Granny loves cats.'

Granny does love cats, but she doesn't love Fatty. When Fatty glares and hisses at my *real* granny, she glares and hisses back. Mum obviously forgot this because she looked very happy with my excuse.

PLONK!

'I'm sorry I said you were an alien, Granny,' I said, and plonked Fatty heavily in her lap.

'That's quite all right, dear,' said the alien granny.

Then something strange happened. The old woman started stroking and fussing over Fatty, but instead of biting her fingers and ripping her arms to shreds, the mean old cat rolled on to his back and started *purring*!

Fatty *never* purrs, except when he's eating or torturing mice or birds or bugs!

'Now we have that silly alien business

sorted out,' Mum said cheerily, 'I
think we should all have a nice slice of
chocolate cake!'

I sat on my beanbag as Mum gathered
up the teacups, but she only got halfway
across the room before the old woman
reached inside her handbag, pulled out
a silver ray gun and zapped her on
the spot!

'ARRRRRGH!'
I yelled, leaping
behind the beanbag
for cover.

'Oh, don't
get your knickers in a twist,' laughed
the alien, shoving Fatty off her lap with
a disapproving grunt. 'Your mother is
perfectly fine. She's just on pause.'

Fatty landed with a thud and stomped
off in a sulk, slinking between the
legs of my paused parent, while Mum
looked like she was playing a game of
musical statues
on her own.

'Why did you put her on pause?' I asked, cautiously leaving my beanbag barricade to make sure Mum was OK. I stepped around her and waved my hand in front of her face. Mum did look fine – she just looked like a waxwork model of Mum.

'I thought you and I should have a little chat,' said the alien, brushing the cat hairs from her dress. 'My planet sent me here to study

families for our *Earth Encyclopaedia*, and I'd be in a lot of trouble if I got found out.'

'I *knew* it!' I said, sitting back down. 'Where's my *real* granny?'

'Your grandmother is fine,' said the alien. 'She phoned your mother last night to say she couldn't make it this weekend. But I intercepted the call while orbiting the planet in my flying saucer.'

'How did you fool her?' I said. 'Granny would know it wasn't Mum –'

'GO TO YOUR ROOM IMMEDIATELY!' yelled the alien, and then smiled proudly.

The voice that came out of her mouth sounded exactly like Mum, which was pretty impressive and also a bit scary.

'I see,' I said. 'And how did you know what my granny looks like?'

'Oh, I've been watching your family through my telescope for a while,' she explained, 'waiting for an opportunity to come down and study you up close, to see what it's like to be part of an Earth family.'

'Aliens don't study cows, then?' I asked.

'No,' said the alien. 'We used to, until

 we realized they're really boring.'

'Can I see your flying saucer?' I asked. Because aside from lying to my granny, stealing her identity and zapping Mum with her ray gun, the alien seemed quite friendly.

'It's hidden very deep in the woods,' she said. 'There's no time for a tour.'

'Can't you just use the teleport machine?' I suggested. Because I've seen loads of sci-fi shows with spaceships, and people beam themselves all over the place and it takes no time at all.

'What's a teleport machine?' asked the alien.

'When you press a button and get beamed up,' I said.

'No, I don't have one of those,' said the alien, looking at the Mum statue and then at her watch. 'Anyway, your mother is only on pause for a few minutes. She'll be back to normal in a moment.'

'Can't you zap her with the ray gun again?' I suggested, because Mum looked

happy enough as a shop dummy and I
really wanted to see the inside of a flying
saucer.

'Sorry, it can only be used for short
periods. Humans get suspicious if they
lose more than a few minutes of time,'
said the alien, slipping the ray gun back
in her handbag. 'And
I was rather looking
forward to sampling
your earthling
chocolate cake.'

I was about to
make another
plea for the
flying saucer
tour when
Mum's tray

of cups rattled. Then she
continued walking across
the room as if nothing
had happened and
disappeared into
the kitchen.

'That was
amazing!'
I gasped.
'I wish I had a ray gun like that!'

The alien granny chuckled and then
leaned forward in her chair.

'So you're not going to give me up to your mum?' she whispered.

'No, I guess not,' I said, thinking that getting to meet a real alien was pretty cool. 'I can imagine her reaction if I said you had a ray gun in your handbag because you're making an *Earth Encyclopaedia*.'

The alien heaved a sigh of relief and sat back in the chair.

'So what do you want to know about human families?' I asked.

The alien asked some questions about my family and I thought my answers were as boring as cows, but she seemed really interested.

Then Mum returned with the cake and the alien scoffed three big slices in

 the time it took me
to eat one.

When the cake
was gone Mum
started talking at
a hundred miles
an hour again,
so I didn't get a
chance to ask the
alien any questions about *alien* families
or the planet *she* came from. I could also
tell she was getting the
rest of the info
she needed
from Mum,
so I felt
pretty
left out.

I couldn't sleep that night because Fatty was back on my laundry bin, snoring his head off – I think he was doing it deliberately because I'd used him as bait. So as I was wide awake anyway, I decided to sneak out and look for the flying saucer!

I jumped the fence at the bottom of the garden and shone my torch into the woods. There were a few snapped branches overhead and on the ground I saw V-shaped footprints from the scuttling saucer! I followed the

footprints as they zigzagged through the
trees until they came to an abrupt halt
in a clearing.

I put my hands out in front of me, just
in case the ship had an invisible button
for camouflage, and walked forward.
In the centre of the clearing I shone the
torch all around the trees and bushes,
but found nothing.

There was only one way the spaceship

could have gone, and that was up!

I looked up and sure enough the flying saucer was hovering a metre over my head. Its lights were off, but it buzzed and wobbled above me like a giant lampshade. It was the coolest thing I'd ever seen!

I was trying to think
of a way to get up there
when I heard a strange
noise coming from the
woods. It sounded like a
stalking animal – and
I was the only prey
around!

'GRRR!' it went.

I shone my torch into the rustling
trees, but the creature was hidden.

'GRRRRRR!' it went again,
closer this time.

Suddenly there was a
rush of movement in a
nearby bush and Fatty shot
out, flying through the air
like a cat-shaped rocket!

'MEAAAW!' he shrieked, shooting
straight at the spaceship and landing
with a mighty *CLANG*!

Fatty was clinging to the edge of the
flying saucer with one front paw and
swiping with the other. The spaceship
looked pretty distressed, spinning and
dipping to shake the attacker loose.

'PUUUUUURRRRRR!' rumbled
Fatty.

It was only when
Fatty started
purring loudly that
I realized what
was happening. He
thought the flying saucer was a giant
bug! And there's nothing that cat likes
more than torturing bugs!

'Stop it!' I yelled. 'Bad moggie!'

I tried to reach up and grab him,
but the flying saucer was lurching
around and kicking its metal legs wildly.
Suddenly Fatty took a big swipe at the

saucer and it crashed to the ground!

Fatty tapped the fallen spaceship with a wary paw, but when it didn't move he lost interest and strutted back towards the house – looking very pleased with himself for killing a giant bug.

I couldn't understand how Fatty had brought down a flying saucer with one swipe, until I saw the cat-scratch down its side with wires spilling out. The torn metal was as thin as paper and hummed beneath my fingers.

That meant the spaceship still had some life in it.

I ran back through the trees, crept into the house and up to the spare bedroom. The alien granny was sitting in bed making notes in a metal book with a laser-beam pen.

LASER-BEAM PEN

COO

'Fatty attacked your flying saucer!' I whispered urgently.

I took the alien to the fallen ship and spent the whole night holding the torch while she repaired the wires and patched the scratch. It was almost dawn when the flying saucer buzzed back into life, and the alien granny was so relieved that she let me see inside.

I was expecting to see walls of flashing lights and buttons like the spaceships on TV, but all of the controls were on a single silver joystick. The alien unzipped her granny disguise and took a seat in the cockpit. She wasn't thin and green with big black eyes – she was thin and *purple* with big black eyes!

The alien gripped the controls with her thin purple fingers.

'I wonder if we should give her a quick test-flight,' she said with a mischievous smile and still using Granny's voice. 'Just to be on the safe side, of course.'

I was so excited I couldn't speak, so I just nodded eagerly.

'Off we go, then!' she said, and pulled back on the joystick.

The flying saucer immediately
shot up through the trees and
kept on going until the town, and
then the city, and then the country
fell away below us. Soon we were
in outer space and looking at the
whole planet below!

'WOW!' I gasped,
and this book is much
too small to write a big
enough 'WOW!'

THE WHOLE PLANET!

WOW!

It was probably the
biggest 'WOW!' in the
history of the world.

A world I was now gawping at with very wide eyes!

'It seems to be working fine,' said the alien, smiling at the flabbergasted look on my face. 'But I'm afraid we have to get back, or else someone might notice we're missing.'

I nodded reluctantly and pressed my face right up against the window for the

trip down. I don't know how fast we
were going as Earth rushed towards us,
but anyone watching from the ground
would only have seen a tiny blur.

For the rest of that day the alien slept
in her chair and I slept on my beanbag,
while Mum talked at a hundred miles
an hour until it was time for Granny to
leave. As she made her way to the door
Fatty glared and hissed, and the alien

glared and hissed back. Which made me
laugh because it was exactly like
my granny.

The next time my *real* granny came to
visit I told her all about the alien granny
impostor and she enjoyed it even more
than the Viking at the zoo story. So I
knew she was *definitely* my granny!

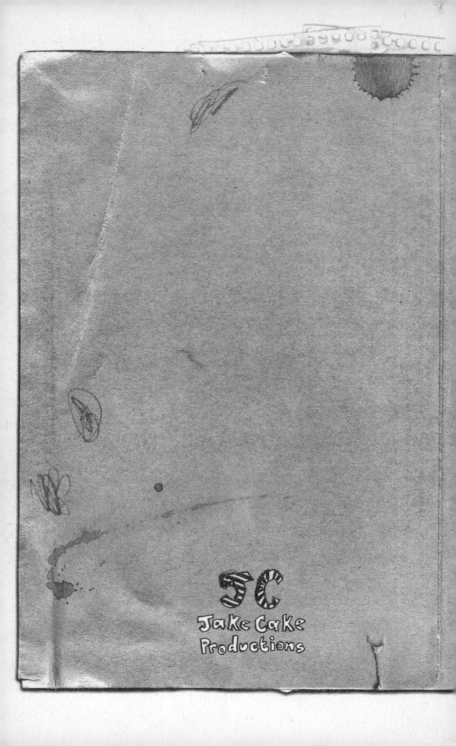

JC

Jake Cake
Productions

I've worked out that when you get into trouble at school there are three things a teacher might say, and it all depends on what you've done and how much trouble you're in.

If it's something small they'll say: 'See me after class!'

If it's something quite naughty they'll say: 'I'll see you at break time!'

And if it's something really bad they'll say: 'Go and see the head teacher!'

On a *really* bad day you can get all three, one after another. Especially if it's a new teacher on their first day and you don't know how strict they are. And there's only one way to find that out for sure . . .

'Jake Cake!' yelled Mrs Snip. 'Have you fallen asleep in my class?'

'No, Miss,' I lied, yawning and propping myself up on the desk. Mrs Snip was our new maths teacher. The last one was Mrs Beady who turned into a werewolf when I fell asleep in *her* class

– but I'll tell you about that another time.

'I distinctly saw your eyes closed!' Mrs Snip snapped. 'See me after class!'

'But I was working out some maths in my head!' I lied again.

'Really?' Mrs Snip narrowed her eyes. 'And what, pray tell, was the answer to this mind-boggling mathematical equation?'

'Er . . . one,' I said, because it was the first number that popped into my head.

'What an amusing coincidence!' Mrs Snip chuckled. 'That's exactly how many break times you'll be spending with me, for falling asleep in class *and* telling a fib.'

'Uh?' I gasped, sitting up straight and feeling very wide awake all of a sudden, which never happens in maths class because maths is the most boring subject ever.

'Do you have something else you wish to add?' asked Mrs Snip.

The way she said it sounded like a warning. 'Or can we get back to the fascinating world of fractions?'

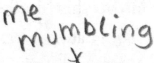

'If fractions *were* fascinating I wouldn't have fallen asleep,' I mumbled.

98

There was a gasp from the rest of the class that made me think that I hadn't mumbled as quietly as I'd hoped, and to confirm this I looked up to see Mrs Snip pointing at the door.

'Go and see the head teacher!' she said firmly.

 Slouching down the corridor I tried to work out how I'd gone from 'See me after class!' to 'Go and see the head teacher!' in such a short space of time.

It seemed a bit fishy, until I remembered that new teachers *always* make their first punishment really harsh as a warning to the rest of the class.

'Typical!' I thought. 'I've just done Mrs Snip a favour!'

Outside the head teacher's office Mrs Price explained that Mr Barton was in a meeting all morning and did not want to be disturbed. Mrs Price is the head

teacher's secretary and therefore knows me quite well.

'So, let me guess,' she said. 'You're in trouble again?'

'Well, I fell asleep in maths class because maths is really boring, and then I said I *hadn't* fallen asleep and that I was doing sums in my head, which wasn't *entirely* true . . .' I paused for a quick breath. 'Then I mumbled something about

 fascinating
fractions,
but it wasn't
a very good
mumble
because
everyone
heard it and Mrs Snip sent me here.'

'Gosh!' said Mrs Price. 'You *have* had
a busy morning.'

I shrugged and tried to look like an
innocent victim of maths.

'Rather than interrupting Mr Barton,
I think *I* should give you something
to do as punishment,' Mrs Price said,
drumming her fingers on the desk
thoughtfully. 'And I *have* noticed the
school trophies are looking a little dull.'

Mrs Price used her key to unlock the big old trophy case in the corridor and armed me with a pair of cleaning cloths and a tin of metal polish. Then she gave me a quick demonstration that involved rubbing the polish on and rubbing the polish off.

'Easy,' I said, thinking it was a bit of a cheek asking me to clean stuff, but it was probably better than facing Mr Barton and *definitely* better than sitting in maths class with strict Mrs Snip.

'And I suggest you use this time to think about telling fibs,' said Mrs Price, heading back to her office. 'Because telling stories that are not true will make your nose grow long.'

'So I've heard,' I sighed.

As I began polishing the trophies I did what Mrs Price suggested and spent a couple of minutes thinking about telling fibs. Mostly I was thinking how strange it was to be in trouble for something I actually *did* this time, and *not* for something unbelievable.

'Makes a nice change!' I said, reaching for a weird silver lamp that looked like a squashed teapot and giving it a good firm rub with the cloth –

RUB! RUB!

BANG!

Suddenly I was standing in a cloud of orange smoke and as I flapped the cloth to clear the air I realized I was no longer alone in the corridor. There was a strange man standing over me!

'ARRRGGGH!'
I yelled.
'ARRRGGGH?'
replied the man.

As the air cleared
I noticed there was
only *half* a strange
man standing over
me because his body
kind of stopped
at the waist. And

hc wasn't really *standing* because his bottom half was made of smoke, and the smoke was trailing out of the weird silver lamp.

'You're a genie!' I gasped, knowing that only genies come out of old lamps.

'Yes I am, and you have released me!' he said, stretching his arms high and groaning like my dad does after he's fallen asleep in the armchair. 'I've been imprisoned in that terrible lamp for a thousand years!'

I could have spent five minutes being freaked out by the sudden appearance of a genie, or run to Mrs Price's office and explained that a person had popped out of one of the trophies. I could also have asked the genie lots of dumb questions about missing legs and lamps and prisons.

But instead I cut straight to the important bit.

'Can I have three wishes?' I asked because that's what genies are famous for.

CLICK!

'Well, of course,' said the genie, and clicked his fingers.

Suddenly there was a wet thud behind me. I looked round to find three dead haddock splattered on the wooden floor, and by the smell wafting up I could tell they were none too fresh!

'YUCK!' I said, holding my nose. 'Where did they come from?'

'You asked for three fishes,' said the genie, scratching his shiny bald head. Actually his head wasn't completely bald because it had

a weird ponytail on top that bobbed
around when he spoke.

'Wishes!' I said. 'I asked for *wishes*,
not *fishes*!'

'Oh,' smirked the genie. 'Sorry, I
don't do wishes.'

'You *don't* do wishes but you *do* do
fishes?' I asked suspiciously.

'I'm what's known as a *mean* genie,'
explained the genie, folding his arms

across his chest majestically. 'Which means you have to grant *me* three wishes if you want to get rid of me!'

'Me?' I gasped. 'I can't grant wishes; I'm just a boy.'

'Have you ever tried?' asked the genie.

'Well, no.' I frowned. 'But . . .'

'Then how do you know you can't?' The genie looked at the trophy case, ran his finger along a dusty shield and pulled a face.

'This dust and grime displeases me. I wish it were clean,' he said, and then looked at me expectantly.

'What?' I said.

'Grant the wish, boy!' he snapped impatiently.

I looked around to make sure no one was watching. Then I turned to the display case, folded my arms like a genie and focused all my attention on granting the wish.

Needless to say nothing happened and I felt pretty silly.

'Try clicking your fingers,' the genie prompted. 'That always works for me.'

I clicked my fingers and still nothing happened. Though I would have been annoyed if I had cleaned them by wish magic, seeing as I'd already cleaned half of them the hard way with polish and a cloth!

'Words sometimes work,' suggested the genie.

'I wish all the trophies were clean and shiny,' I mumbled half-heartedly.

As quick as a flash the genie clicked his fingers,

a cloud of dust burst from the display case
and when the air cleared, all the silver
trophies were sparkling like diamonds.

'*You* did that!' I said,
thinking he
was trying
to fool me
into believing I'd
done it myself.

'Of course,' said
the genie. 'You wished for clean trophies
and I granted it.'

'But that was *your* wish!' I said, 'That's
what *you* asked *me* for.'

'Are you a genie?' asked the genie,
viewing my legs with suspicion.

'You know I'm not a genie,' I yelled.
'You said you didn't do wishes because

you were a
mean genie
and that I
had to
grant –'
  'I lied,'
said the

genie, and then roared with laughter.

  'So you're not a mean genie?' I
growled.

  'Oh, I'm mean and a genie,' he
explained. 'But I still have to grant three
wishes because those're the rules.'

  'So I *do* have three wishes?' I gasped.

  'Well, you *did* have three wishes,' he
corrected. 'But now you only have one.'

  'One?' I said. 'But I haven't even
asked for anything.'

The genie slipped
on a pair of
glasses,
pulled
a small
notebook
from the
pocket
of his waistcoat and flicked through the
pages in a very businesslike fashion.
Then he stopped and prodded the page
with a pencil.

'My wish records show "three fishes at
10.45 a.m.",' he said, nodding towards
the pile of stinking haddock. 'And "clean
trophies at 10.50 a.m.",' he added,
jabbing a thumb at the trophy case.
'Which leaves how many?'

I did the sum in my head and arrived at a familiar number.

'One,' I growled, angry that I'd been tricked *and* was getting a maths lesson!

The genie smiled mischievously as the glasses, notebook and pencil vanished into thin air.

I realized I'd have to watch what I said if I stood any chance of getting the last wish granted on something good. The genie was as slippery as the haddock!

I thought about asking for a million *more* wishes, but after what happened with the first wish I didn't want to be

surrounded by a million fishes. The
three on the floor smelled bad enough!

'I want a hover bike that can travel
through time,' I said, after giving it a lot
of thought.

'And
when I say
"bike" I don't
mean "fish"
and when I say
"time" I don't
mean "fish".'

'Does such a time-travel hover bike exist?' asked the genie.

'Well, no,' I said. 'Not exactly, but –'

'I'm afraid I can only grant wishes for things that exist in the *real* world. Like a nice toy car, for example!' A small plastic car appeared in his hand with a *pop*. 'VROOM! VROOM!' he said, spinning its wheels excitedly.

VRoom! VRoom!

'I'm not four years old!' I said.

'Would you *like* to be four years old?' asked the genie with a wicked grin.

'*NO!*' I gasped.

The car disappeared and was replaced with a clock. The genie gazed at it and then sighed wearily.

'Don't rush me,' I said.

I racked my brains for something I really wanted — which would have been a lot easier without a mean genie huffing and puffing impatiently.

It was then that I saw Mrs Snip through the windows of the double doors. She was at the other end of the

corridor and heading in my direction. The look on her face was very fierce.

'I wish I wasn't in trouble!' I blurted out.

dull-sounding
CLICK

The genie clicked his fingers, and then frowned at the dull-sounding click.

'You're not *in* trouble,' he said. 'I can't undo something that isn't there.'

'Is this another trick?' I asked, because the look on Mrs Snip's face as she approached the doors said I was in a lot of trouble indeed. Then I saw the fish and panicked again. 'Get rid of the fish!'

'Done!' said the genie, and with a sharp click the fish immediately vanished. 'Now I've granted three wishes, I'm out of here!' he added, folding his arms across his chest and staring with purpose at the lamp.

'Where are you going?' I gasped.

'Back inside my lamp, of course!' said the genie.

'But you said the lamp was a terrible prison!'

'Ah, that was a bit of a fib too. It's actually a palace, with satin cushions and gold plates and servants,' said the genie. 'And best of all there are no angry teachers to tell you what to do.'

'Can I come?' I said.

'No room, sorry!' and with this the genie nodded and dissolved into a cloud of orange smoke. The smoke whirled

in the air like a mini tornado and snaked its way back inside the lamp.

Just then Mrs Snip burst through the double doors

and found
me staring at
the lamp with
my mouth
hanging
open. As
she stormed
down the

corridor I rubbed the
metal frantically with
my sleeve.

'Get back out
here!' I growled.

'Who are you
talking to?' Mrs Snip
demanded, but before

I could say anything she waved her question away with a flapping hand.

'Actually, don't answer that. I've heard all about your *wild* imagination and I'd hate to see you get into trouble.'

'But I'm already in trouble,' I said, thinking Mrs Snip had the memory of a goldfish. 'For falling asleep in class and telling a fib and saying fractions aren't fascinating.'

'Well, you *were* a
bit cheeky,' chuckled
Mrs Snip. Her stern
expression vanished like
the genie into his lamp
and she seemed quite
friendly all of a sudden.
'But you're not *really*
in trouble. In fact I'm
terribly grateful to you.'

'Uh?' I said, wondering what she
was going on about.
Then I did another
quick sum in my
head and realized I'd
worked it out earlier.
'You sent me to
the head teacher

so everyone would think you're *strict*!'

'I'm afraid so.' Mrs Snip sighed guiltily. 'You see, in my last school I was known as a bit of a softie, and I couldn't teach properly because no one ever behaved in my classroom.'

'That's hard to believe,' I mumbled.

'Then it worked!' gasped Mrs Snip, looking very relieved.

'But you sent me to the *head teacher*!' I said, thinking Mrs Snip might be as slippery as the genie *and* his slimy fishes. 'I would have been in REAL trouble if Mr Barton had seen me!'

'Oh, don't worry. I knew the head teacher was in a meeting all morning.' Mrs Snip smiled reassuringly. 'I never would have sent you here if I thought you'd be punished, and I didn't think you'd mind missing a bit of the lesson.'

'Mrs Price made me clean the trophies,' I grumbled.

'Oh dear,' said Mrs Snip, shifting uncomfortably. 'That's very unfortunate.'

'So I'm *not* in trouble?' I said, placing the lamp back inside the trophy case and closing the glass door. 'Even though I fell asleep and fibbed and said fractions weren't fascinating?'

'Not if you agree to return to class with a very sorry look on your face, and promise to keep my secret,' she said hopefully, holding out a hand to shake. 'Do we have a deal?'

I thought about it for a moment and decided that being the only kid who knew Mrs Snip was a big softie was a pretty cool position to be in, and might come in handy next time I fell asleep in maths class.

'No homework for a month?' I said, thinking I deserved a bit of

compensation after all the trouble
I'd had with the mean genie, and for
making me panic *and* waste my last
wish.

'A week?' said Mrs Snip. 'And I
promise to make the maths more
interesting.'

'Deal!' I said, shaking her hand firmly.

'Now tell me, Jake,' said Mrs Snip,
waving her hand in front of her nose
as we walked back down the corridor.
'Does this school *always* smell of rotten
haddock?'

'Only when something *fishy* is going
on,' I said.

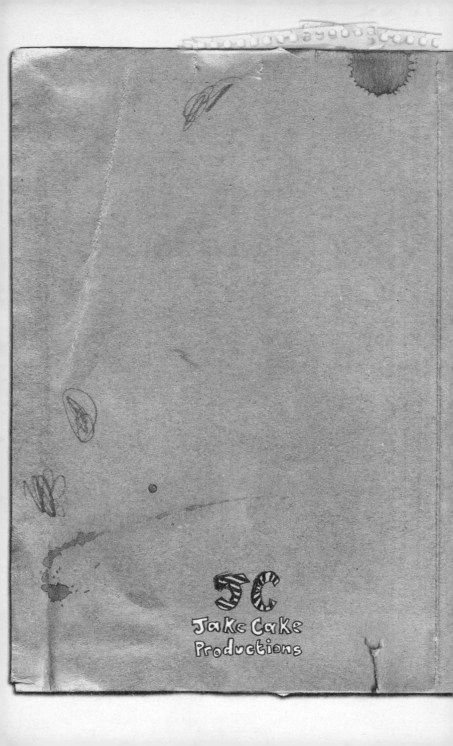

JC
Jake Cake
Productions

UNBELIEVABLE ADVENTURE REPORT

OFFICIAL JC DOCUMENT

NAME: Old Crusty (or Captain Crusty)

AGE: Probably a couple of hundred years old!

HEIGHT: Nothing cos he's a ghost

How To Spot One. Find a treasure chest with barnacles! ~~barnacles Barnacles~~

Comments: I really liked Old Crusty (and his parrot). Now he's sailing the SEVEN seas in a yacht or a speed boat so you might see him in one of those. Pirates really like chocolate.

JC

Jake Cake Productions

mr Crooke doesn't! He He

UNBELIEVABLE ADVENTURE REPORT

NAME: Alien

AGE: I didn't get a chance to ask

WEIGHT: not much cos she was very thin.

How To Spot One Look up! (or look closely at your granny!)

Comments: The alien I met was great and I would still like to have my own RAY GUN to pause people. The flying Saucer ride was the COOLEST thing EVER!

JC Jake Cake Productions

OFFICIAL JC DOCUMENT

NAME: Mean Genie

AGE: Over a thousand years old cos he was in the lamp that long.

WEIGHT: Not sure – probably nothing.

How To Spot One rub a lamp!

Comments: Genies are very sneaky and they try to trick you out of getting your wishes. So be very careful or you might end up with a pile of rotten haddock!

JC
Jake Cake
Productions

YUCK!

Read all the unbelievable adventures of

JAKE CAKE

that's me →

I did all the writing and all the drawing

puffin.co.uk